Phonics Friends

Taejon and Terrel
The Sound of T

The
Child's
World

By Cecilia Minden and Joanne Meier

The Child's World®

Published in the United States of America
by The Child's World®
PO Box 326
Chanhassen, MN 55317-0326
800-599-READ
www.childsworld.com

A special thank you to Mrs. Bedar, principal of Shoesmith
Elementary School, for allowing us the opportunity to
photograph students, and to Jane Robinson, for making
it all possible.

The Child's World®: Mary Berendes, Publishing Director

Editorial Directions, Inc.: E. Russell Primm, Editorial Director
and Project Editor; Katie Marsico, Associate Editor; Judith
Shiffer, Associate Editor and School Media Specialist;
Linda S. Koutris, Photo Researcher and Selector

The Design Lab: Kathleen Petelinsek, Design and Page
Production

Photographs ©: Photo setting and photography by Romie
and Alice Flanagan/Flanagan Publishing Services: cover,
4, 10, 12, 14, 16, 18, 20; Corbis: 6; Corbis/Donna
Disario: 8.

Library of Congress Cataloging-in-Publication Data
Minden, Cecilia.
  Taejon and Terrel : the sound of T / by Cecilia Minden
and Joanne Meier.
    p. cm. — (Phonics friends)
  Summary: Simple text featuring the sound of the letter "t"
describes how brothers Taejon and Terrel like to play
together.
  ISBN 1-59296-306-4 (library bound : alk. paper)
  [1. English language—Phonetics. 2. Reading.] I. Meier,
Joanne D. II. Title. III. Series.
  PZ7.M6539Tae 2004
  [E]—dc22
                                        2004003540

Note to parents and educators:

The Child's World® has created Phonics Friends with the goal of exposing children to engaging stories and pictures that assist in phonics development. The books in the series will help children learn the relationships between the letters of written language and the individual sounds of spoken language. This contact helps children learn to use these relationships to read and write words.

The books in this series follow a similar format. An introductory page, to be read by an adult, introduces the child to the phonics feature, or sound, that will be highlighted in the book. Read this page to the child, stressing the phonic feature. Help the student learn how to form the sound with her mouth. The Phonics Friends story and engaging photographs follow the introduction. At the end of the story, word lists categorize the feature words into their phonic element. Additional information on using these lists is on The Child's World® Web site listed at the top of this page.

Each book in this series has been carefully written to meet specific readability requirements. Close attention has been paid to elements such as word count, sentence length, and vocabulary. Readability formulas measure the ease with which the text can be read and understood. Each Phonics Friends book has been analyzed using the Spache readability formula. For more information on this formula, as well as the levels for each of the books in this series please visit The Child's World® Web site.

Reading research suggests that systematic phonics instruction can greatly improve students' word recognition, spelling, and comprehension skills. The Phonics Friends series assists in the teaching of phonics by providing students with important opportunities to apply their knowledge of phonics as they read words, sentences, and text.

This is the letter *t*.

In this book, you will read words that have the *t* sound as in:

toy, tag, team, and *teacher.*

Taejon and Terrel are brothers.

They like to do things together.

They play toy trains.

They climb trees.

They ride on the tire swing.

They like to play tag.

They play on the same team.

Taejon is number ten.

Terrel is number two.

They take turns kicking the ball.

They have the same teacher.

Her name is Miss Topper.

Which one is Terrel?

Which one is Taejon?

Taejon is tall.

Terrel has a missing tooth.

It is fun to be brothers together.

Fun Facts

Do you like sports? If the answer is yes, then you probably have played on a team at some point. In baseball, nine members of each team are on the field during a play. In football and field hockey, that number is eleven, and in basketball, it is five.

Have you ever lost a tooth? All kids lose about 20 primary teeth (also called baby teeth) between the ages of 5 and 13. By adulthood, most people have a set of 32 permanent teeth. This is less than several other creatures, including dogs and pigs. Dogs have 42 teeth, and pigs have 44.

Activity

Relay Racing with Two Teams

Do you enjoy racing? If so, invite your friends over for a day of relay races. You will need to divide into two teams. Races might include running from one point to another, dribbling a basketball between two plastic cones, or even hopping back and forth in a potato sack! Members of the winning team get to decide what the next relay race will be. Be sure to take breaks between races and to drink plenty of water so you stay energized.

To Learn More

Books
About the Sound of T
Klingel, Cynthia, and Robert B. Noyed. *Task Time: The Sound of T.* Chanhassen, Minn.: The Child's World, 2000.

About Teams
Brown, Marc Tolon. *Arthur Makes the Team.* Boston: Little, Brown and Co., 1998.
Golenbock, Peter, and Paul Bacon (illustrator). *Teammates.* San Diego: Harcourt Brace Jovanovich, 1990.

About Teeth
Clement, Rod. *Grandpa's Teeth.* New York: HarperCollins, 1997.
Simms, Laura, and David Catrow (illustrator). *Rotten Teeth.* Boston: Houghton Mifflin, 1998.

About Togetherness
Holzschuher, Cynthia. *Play Together, Share Together: Fun Activities for Parents and Children.* Westminster, Calif.: Teacher Created Materials, 2000.
Lobel, Arnold. *Frog and Toad Together.* New York: Harper and Row, 1972.

Web Sites
Visit our home page for lots of links about the Sound of T:

http://www.childsworld.com/links.html

Note to Parents, Teachers, and Librarians: We routinely check our Web links to make sure they're safe, active sites—so encourage your readers to check them out!

T Feature Words

Proper Names
Taejon
Terrel
Topper

Feature Words in Initial Position
tag
take
tall
teacher
team
ten
tire
to
together
tooth
toy
turn
two

Feature Words with Blends
train
tree

About the Authors

Cecilia Minden, PhD, directs the Language and Literacy Program at the Harvard Graduate School of Education. She is a reading specialist with classroom and administrative experience in grades K–12. She earned her PhD in reading education from the University of Virginia. Cecilia and her husband Dave Cupp enjoy sharing their love of reading with their granddaughter Chelsea.

Joanne Meier, PhD, has worked as an elementary school teacher and university professor. She earned her BA in early childhood education from the University of South Carolina, and her MEd and PhD in education from the University of Virginia. She currently works as a literacy consultant for schools and private organizations. Joanne Meier lives with her husband Eric, and spends most of her time chasing her two daughters, Kella and Erin, and her two cats, Sam and Gilly, in Charlottesville, Virginia.